Tere Baad

Prashant Bhardwaj

Published by Prashant Bhardwaj, 2025.

This is a work of fiction. Similarities to real people, places, or events are entirely coincidental.

TERE BAAD

First edition. October 8, 2025.

ISBN: 979-8232348816

Written by Prashant Bhardwaj.

Table of Contents

To those who have loved deeply and lost,To the hearts that have been broken yet continue to hope,And to the ones who remind us that even after the darkest moments,Life has a way of offering a second chance.

"After every ending comes a beginning we never saw coming."

Tere
Baad
Prashant Bhardwaj

TERE BAAD

(A Tale of Broken Hearts & New Beginnings)

"Every ending whispers a new beginning... after you."

"A novel by Prashant Bhardwaj"

Chapter 1 – A New Beginning

The office buzzed softly with the rhythm of keyboards and hushed conversations. Arav sat at his desk, his eyes fixed on the glowing screen, fingers moving steadily across the keyboard. Work had become his shield—every line of code, every deadline, another wall he built between himself and a world he no longer trusted.

A familiar hand appeared beside him, holding out a steaming cup of tea.

"Here, brother. Tea," Ram said with a grin as he pulled a chair next to him. Ram was the only colleague Arav had allowed close, the only one who had managed to break through his silence.

Arav accepted the cup with a slight nod. "Thanks."

Ram studied him for a moment before shaking his head. "Why are you always so serious? This is an office, not a prison."

Arav gave a faint smile. "I just prefer to keep my focus on work."

Ram sipped his own tea, leaning back comfortably. "You've cut yourself off from the world more than from work. You don't even talk to any of the girls here. Come on, man, live a little."

Arav's hands froze on the keyboard. His gaze drifted to the tea in his hand, the rising steam blurring his reflection in the cup. After a pause, he said quietly, "After what happened in the past... I stopped letting myself break. Even friendship—I only keep it with people who truly understand."

Ram's expression softened. He placed a hand on Arav's shoulder. "Time heals every wound, brother. Just give yourself some."

Arav didn't reply. He looked out of the window instead, where Mumbai's skyline stretched endlessly—tall, bright, and indifferent. Somewhere in the chaos of this city, he hoped he might find himself again.

Chapter 2 – The First Impression

The office was unusually lively that morning. Laughter echoed through the cubicles as boxes of sweets passed from desk to desk. It was Sana's birthday, and she moved through the rows of colleagues, smiling brightly as each one wished her.

"Happy Birthday, Sana!"

"God bless you!"

"Many happy returns!"

Her face glowed with warmth as she handed out sweets, one by one, until finally she reached Arav's desk.

"Here," she said softly, offering him a piece of barfi.

Arav looked up for a brief moment, then shook his head. "I don't like sweets." His voice was calm but dismissive.

Before the silence grew heavy, Ram, who stood beside Arav, quickly stepped in. "I'll take it! Thanks, Sana." He grinned, trying to lighten the moment.

Sana gave a polite smile and moved on, but inside, she couldn't help feeling a sting. Everyone else wished me, but not him. How arrogant... how rude.

Throughout the day, she noticed Arav again and again. While others chatted, laughed, and took small breaks, Arav remained at his desk—eyes fixed on his work, shoulders stiff, completely shut off from the world. He doesn't even try, she thought, a mixture of irritation and curiosity filling her mind.

By evening, the office emptied as people rushed home. Sana gathered her bag, only to notice Arav still at his desk, typing away, untouched by the clock. She shook her head slightly and walked out.

But outside, the city wasn't kind that day. A strike had left rickshaws and buses scarce, forcing her to walk home. The streets grew quieter as she passed a dimly lit lane. On the roadside, a group of men smoked and drank, their eyes narrowing the moment they saw her.

"Pretty girl walking alone," one of them muttered. They rose, circling closer.

Sana's heart raced. Fear surged through her veins as she clutched her bag tighter and quickened her pace. When their footsteps followed, she broke into a run.

Her breath came in sharp bursts as she dashed back toward the main road. And then, ahead of her, she saw him—Arav, standing near a tea stall. Relief washed over her instantly.

"Arav!" she cried, running to him. "Please help me! They're chasing me!"

Arav's brows knit in concern. "What happened? Why are you running like this?"

Before she could answer, the goons swaggered up behind her. One of them sneered. "Step aside, hero. This girl is ours."

Arav's calm expression hardened. His voice was quiet, but each word cut sharp. "She is not a thing to be owned. She belongs to no one."

The man laughed and moved closer—until Arav's fist crashed into his jaw. Another tried to grab Sana, but Arav spun, delivering a powerful kick to his ribs. The third lunged, only to be thrown to the ground with a brutal twist. Within moments, the lane echoed with groans of defeat.

Sana trembled, tears threatening to spill. "Thank you... you saved me. You saved my dignity."

Arav brushed the dust from his hands, his voice steady. "It's not a big deal. No woman should ever have to face this." He looked at her gently. "It's late. Come with me—I'll drop you home."

For the first time, Sana saw something beyond his cold exterior. The man she thought was rude and egoistic was the same man who had just fought for her dignity. And somewhere deep inside, a new thought began to stir.

Chapter 3 – The Wound Beneath

The office canteen buzzed with the usual morning chatter—the clinking of cups, the faint hiss of the coffee machine, colleagues laughing over small jokes. Sana sat across from Ram at a corner table, stirring her tea absentmindedly. Her mind wasn't on the drink, though. It was still replaying last night—those terrifying moments on the street, and how Arav had stepped in, fighting for her without hesitation.

Yet the memory of yesterday morning lingered too. How coldly he had refused her birthday sweet. How he never smiled, never spoke more than a few words. She couldn't reconcile the two images—the rude, distant colleague and the fearless protector.

Finally, she blurted out, "Ram... why is Arav always like this? So arrogant, so closed off. He behaves as if the world doesn't exist."

Ram looked at her thoughtfully, setting down his cup. "He's not arrogant, Sana. Just... wounded."

"Wounded?" she asked, her brows knitting in surprise.

Ram leaned forward, lowering his voice as if sharing something heavy. "He went through a heartbreak. A bad one. He gave everything he had—his love, his trust, his dreams. And in return... he was betrayed."

Sana's spoon stilled in her cup. She felt an unexpected ache at his words. "Betrayed?"

Ram nodded. "After that, he stopped letting people in. He doesn't trust easily anymore. Work is all he has left. It's his way of surviving."

Sana looked down, her chest tightening. For the first time, she saw beyond Arav's coldness. His silence wasn't ego. His distance wasn't pride. It was pain—hidden deep, but strong enough to keep the world at arm's length.

And she couldn't help but wonder: What kind of heartbreak leaves a man like that?

Chapter 4 – An Unspoken Bond

After realizing that Arav was not an arrogant or egoistic man but someone carrying the wounds of a broken love, Sana found herself thinking about him the whole day. His silence and rudeness now made sense to her. She couldn't help but feel a strange pull toward him, a mixture of curiosity and concern.

That evening, as most of the staff began leaving the office, Sana noticed Arav still sitting at his desk. Gathering a little courage, she walked up to him.

"You're not going home?" she asked softly.

Arav didn't respond. He kept looking at the files in front of him as if he hadn't heard her.

• • ✤ • •

SANA ASKED AGAIN, A little louder, "Don't you want to go home?"

Finally, Arav looked up. "I have work to finish. Why are you asking? Have you completed your work?"

"Yes, I'm done," Sana replied.

"Then why are you still here? Don't get late. Go home," Arav said, his tone calm but distant.

Sana raised her hands playfully, trying to lighten the mood. "Okay, okay, I'm going. Don't be angry." She took a step back, then added warmly, "Thank you."

Arav frowned slightly. "Why are you thanking me?"

• • ✤ • •

"FOR SAVING ME FROM those goons the other day," she said, her voice carrying a touch of shyness.

Arav nodded once, not saying more. Sana smiled faintly and left.

After some time, Arav too left the office and rode away on his bike. The night air was cool, the roads nearly empty. Suddenly, he noticed someone standing by the roadside. It was Sana, waiting for a bus. She spotted him as well and immediately waved her hands in the air, signaling for a lift.

Arav stopped the bike in front of her. "What happened? Why did you stop me?" he asked, though he already knew the answer.

"I've been waiting for the bus. It's too late... will you please drop me?" Sana said, almost pleading.

Arav hesitated. "No, I can't." He started his bike again and began to leave.

But in the side mirror, he caught sight of her face—sad, innocent, almost childlike. Something stirred in his heart. With a deep sigh, he turned the bike around and went back to her.

He stopped silently in front of her.

"What happened?" Sana asked in surprise.

"It's too late," Arav said quietly. "I'll drop you... but only this one time."

Sana's lips curved into a relieved smile. "Okay," she replied softly.

• • • •

SHE SAT BEHIND HIM, and together they rode into the night, the unspoken bond between them slowly beginning to form.

Chapter 5 – The Business Trip

The next morning, the company boardroom buzzed with anticipation. Executives and staff filled the long polished table, their voices low as they speculated about the unexpected meeting. The atmosphere shifted the moment the CEO entered, his confident stride commanding silence.

"I have an important announcement," he began, his tone steady but charged with energy. "A major international project has come to us from Japan. After careful consideration, I've decided that Arav will lead this project."

Murmurs rippled through the room. Every eye turned toward Arav. Calm and composed, he rose slightly from his chair and gave a respectful nod.

"Thank you, sir," he said simply.

The CEO's gaze softened, filled with pride. "I chose you because of your spirit and your hard work for this company, Arav. You've earned this. As the head of this project, you have the authority to select the team members who will accompany you on this business trip to Japan."

Arav paused for a moment, thoughtful. Then he spoke with quiet certainty. "The first name I would like to put forward is Ram. He has a solid understanding of the project's details and his insights will be valuable. The second name is Sana. I've seen her dedication and consistency at work, and I believe she will add great strength to the team."

The CEO nodded approvingly. "Very well. It's your call. I'll give you until tomorrow if you wish to make changes to your team. If you decide to replace Ram or Sana, inform me directly. Otherwise, the team stands as is."

• • ❧ • •

ARAV BOWED HIS HEAD slightly. "Understood, sir."

As the meeting adjourned, staff whispered among themselves. Across the room, Anjali had overheard every word. Disappointment flickered in her eyes—she had hoped to be chosen. But as she watched Arav leave the boardroom, her disappointment shifted into determination. If she couldn't be part of the team yet, she would find another way to get closer to him. And the upcoming Japan trip only fueled her resolve.

SCENE 6: OFFICE CAFETERIA – DAY

(Arav is sitting at a corner table with his laptop open, reviewing project notes. Anjali walks in, carrying her coffee, and immediately spots him. She walks over with a big smile, trying to sound casual but clearly eager.)

ANJALI (overly sweet, sitting across from him)

Arav, your Japan presentation is going to be amazing. Honestly, this project would have been impossible without you.

ARAV (eyes still on the laptop, typing)

Thanks, Anjali. Let's just keep the focus on work.

(Anjali's smile falters for a moment, but she quickly composes herself, determined not to give up. She leans in slightly.)

ANJALI

Still, I really admire how dedicated you are. It's inspiring. Maybe... we could discuss some ideas together later?

(Arav finally looks up, his tone polite but distant.)

ARAV

If it's about the project, sure. Otherwise, I don't have much time these days.

(Anjali forces another smile, hiding her disappointment. Just then, Sana enters the cafeteria and quietly observes the interaction from a distance. She notices how hard Anjali is trying to get Arav's attention, and a subtle flicker of concern appears on her face. Sana doesn't say anything yet, but it's clear she has started to take note of Anjali's behavior.)

SANA (V.O. – inner monologue, soft and thoughtful)

Anjali again? She's been hovering around him a lot lately... and Arav doesn't even notice. He's so focused on work. But still... why do I feel uneasy seeing this?

(Camera lingers on Sana's thoughtful expression, hinting at the beginning of her protective feelings for Arav before fading out.)

Chapter 7 – Bridges Beyond Borders

The next morning, Arav, Ram, and Sana were ready for their business trip to Japan. Excitement and anticipation mingled with a sense of responsibility. Sana felt a quiet happiness—Arav hadn't indulged Anjali's attempts to get close, and that simple act of integrity made her admire him even more.

At the airport, after completing the boarding process, they made their way onto the plane. Arav and Ram had seats next to each other, while Sana was seated a little farther away. Her fellow traveler, however, proved to be loud and restless, constantly shifting and speaking without pause. Sana tried to stay composed, but it was obvious she was uncomfortable.

Ram noticed immediately. With a reassuring smile, he said, "Don't worry, Sana. Take my seat—I'll sit there instead."

Grateful, Sana accepted the swap. Now sitting beside Arav, she felt a wave of relief and quiet joy. Arav glanced at her briefly, offered a polite nod, and returned to his work. Though he seemed absorbed in his laptop, the closeness of their seats brought an unspoken warmth that neither of them addressed directly.

The following day, they stepped into the Japanese conference room, their hearts steady but minds focused. Arav led the presentation with confidence, Ram provided precise technical details, and Sana contributed her creative insights with clarity. The Japanese team listened intently, impressed by the seamless collaboration and professionalism of the trio.

When the presentation ended, the room erupted in applause. The Japanese director spoke through a translator, "Your team's vision is strong. This project belongs to you."

It was a moment of triumph.

Chapter 8 – Whispers Beneath the Blossoms

The next day in Japan, Sana and Arav wandered through the serene courtyard of a centuries-old temple. A gentle snowfall dusted the ancient rooftops, while cherry blossoms, still clinging stubbornly to the branches, added delicate splashes of pink against the white. The air was crisp, filled with the faint echo of temple bells.

Sana looked at Arav, a soft smile playing on her lips.

"How do you find this place?" she asked, her voice calm yet curious.

Arav took a moment to take in the tranquility, the stillness that seemed to embrace them both. He looked at her, his expression quiet and sincere.

"Peaceful... just like you," he said.

Her cheeks tinged slightly pink, and she returned his gaze with a gentle smile.

"Every place feels beautiful when I'm with you," she murmured.

As they walked, Sana's thoughts drifted quietly. Why do I feel this way around him? she wondered. It's not just his kindness or calm... it's something deeper. He's different from anyone I've ever met, and I can't stop noticing him, not even for a moment.

For a long while, they moved in harmony beneath the drifting cherry blossoms. The quiet was not awkward—it was comforting, almost sacred, as if the world had slowed down just for the two of them. In that moment, neither needed to speak; the gentle snowfall and soft petals did all the talking.

Chapter 9 – The Night of Confessions

The night was calm in Tokyo, the city lights shimmering like fallen stars across the horizon. Arav stood alone on the balcony of his hotel room, his thoughts restless, his mind weighed down by memories he tried so hard to bury.

The sudden chime of the doorbell startled him. Opening the door, he was surprised to find Sana standing there.

"May I come in?" she asked softly.

"Of course," Arav replied, stepping aside. "What happened? Why are you here this late?"

She hesitated, then smiled apologetically. "Sorry if I disturbed you. I just... I couldn't sleep. And I had this feeling you'd be awake."

Arav raised an eyebrow, curious. "And how exactly did you know that?"

"Because it's your habit," she said gently. "You always work late into the night."

For the first time in hours, a small smile touched his lips.

Sana walked over to the balcony and looked out at the glowing skyline. After a pause, she turned back to him. "Arav... can we be closer friends?"

He looked at her sharply, almost guarded. "Why do you want to be my friend? I'm not... good enough for that."

"Why would you say that?" she frowned. "You're a good person."

Arav's smile faded. His voice carried a bitter edge. "If I was good, then why was I cheated? Why am I still alone? Maybe I don't deserve to be part of anyone's life."

"You're talking nonsense," Sana said firmly, her eyes steady on him. "She left you, right? Then she's the one who didn't deserve you. That doesn't make you bad."

Arav froze, his gaze narrowing. "How do you know about my breakup?"

Sana hesitated before answering, "I asked Ram. He told me a little. Not everything... only that you loved a girl deeply and she walked away. If you don't mind... if you can trust me... maybe sharing your pain will lighten it."

For a moment, Arav stood silent, torn between his walls and her warmth. Then slowly, almost as if the words forced themselves out, he began to tell her everything—how he had met Siya, how love blossomed, and how brutally it ended.

As he spoke, his voice cracked, the weight of unhealed wounds pressing down. His eyes filled with tears. Finally, he sank to his knees, clutching his head.

"Why did she leave me?" he whispered hoarsely. "I loved her more than myself. What was my fault?" His voice broke as he suddenly embraced Sana, seeking solace he hadn't allowed himself in years.

The hug was desperate, raw with emotion. But as the realization struck him, he quickly pulled back, ashamed. "I'm sorry... I shouldn't have... you must think I'm just an emotional fool."

Sana's heart ached at his vulnerability. She shook her head firmly. "No, Arav. You're not a fool. You're kind. You loved her with all your heart, and she failed you. That doesn't make you weak—it makes you real. Let her go. Focus on yourself. Change is the only rule of nature."

Arav looked at her, her words seeping deep into him. For the first time in years, he felt understood. He nodded faintly. "You're right."

The two stood silently side by side on the balcony, the city glittering beneath them. Sana's voice broke the silence, soft and thoughtful.

"Did you ever think you'd trust someone again?"

Arav's answer was quiet, almost a whisper. "No. But you... you've changed everything."

Her heart pounded as she gently reached out, her fingers slipping into his. He didn't resist. Instead, he let her hold his hand, their silence saying what words couldn't.

Chapter 10 – The Unwanted Closeness

The office buzzed with its usual rhythm of ringing phones, hurried footsteps, and the constant hum of typing. But Sana's eyes were fixed only on one corner of the floor—on Arav's desk.

Anjali strolled in with her usual overconfidence, her sharp heels clicking against the tiles. Without hesitation, she leaned over Arav's table.

"Shall we go for lunch?" she asked sweetly, flashing him a carefully practiced smile.

Arav didn't even look up from his work. "Sorry. I have a lot to do."

Sana's lips curled into a soft, almost victorious smile. Good... he said no.

But Anjali wasn't one to accept defeat. She tilted her head, batted her eyelashes, and placed her manicured hand lightly on Arav's shoulder. "Please come. Just a short break. You work too much."

Sana's smile vanished. Her chest tightened, and before she could stop herself, words began spilling out under her breath.

Look at her... just look at the way she's clinging to him. If she had her way, she would swallow him whole. And why is he not saying anything? Why is he just sitting there? Push her away, Arav. Don't let her touch you. Go away from him, Anjali. He's not yours.

Her heart pounded as she watched the scene unfold.

Arav finally sighed and turned his head toward Anjali. Calm but firm, he lifted her hand from his shoulder and placed it aside. "I have a lot of work to do. I can't come with you. So please... go and focus on your own work."

The air seemed to shift. Anjali's smile faltered, her pride slightly bruised, but she covered it with a forced laugh. "Fine. Workaholic!" She walked away, tossing her hair dramatically.

Sana exhaled slowly, relief washing over her like a cool breeze. A tiny smile tugged at her lips again. That's my Arav. He doesn't belong to her.

But deep inside, she knew this was only the beginning of Anjali's persistence. And perhaps, the beginning of her own silent battle.

Chapter 11 – The Proposal at Dusk

The office was winding down for the day. Files were closed, computers were shut off, and the golden hue of the evening sun streamed in through the tall glass windows. Arav packed his laptop bag, ready to leave. He looked tired but content, his eyes reflecting the long hours of dedication he had given to his work.

Across the hall, Anjali stood waiting. She had been watching him for a while, her heart restless with the decision she had made. She wanted a successful man for her husband—someone ambitious, responsible, and stable. In her eyes, Arav was the perfect choice.

Before Sana could walk over to Arav, Anjali stepped forward quickly.

"Arav, I need to say something," she said firmly.

Arav glanced at her, slightly puzzled. "Yes, Anjali, what happened?"

"Not here," she insisted, her eyes glimmering with urgency. "Come with me—somewhere quiet. Just you and me."

Arav frowned and shook his head. "I'm very tired. I can't go anywhere right now."

Just as Anjali's face fell in disappointment, Sana arrived, her timing precise. She had also been waiting for him to finish.

"Arav," she said softly, "can you drop me home, if you don't mind?"

Arav gave her a small nod. "Okay."

The two began walking towards the exit together, but Anjali's voice stopped them.

"Arav!" she called out.

He halted at the office gate, Sana pausing beside him. Anjali approached, her eyes determined, her tone bold.

"I am a straightforward girl," she declared. "I don't like to waste time. I want to tell you something. I like your dedication, your hard work. You are intelligent, handsome... a husband material man."

Before either of them could react, Anjali sank to her knees, holding out her hand. Her voice trembled but carried conviction.

"I love you, Arav. Will you marry me?"

Sana's heart burned. Jealousy and anger twisted inside her chest as she watched Anjali's daring move. Under her breath, she murmured furiously, "I'll kill you, Anjali... go back! Arav, please don't accept her proposal. Please, God, don't let him say yes..."

Arav's face hardened. He took a step forward, his voice sharp.

"Get up, Anjali. Stop acting foolish. That's enough."

Without giving her a chance to argue, he turned to Sana. "Aren't you getting late? Why are you standing like a statue? Do you want to come with me or not?"

Sana blinked quickly, her heart leaping. "Yes—yes, I do. Let's go."

As they walked away, Anjali stood frozen. Arav's rejection struck her pride like a blade. Her hands clenched, her breath uneven.

She had confessed with courage, only to be humiliated.

Her ego flared.

Her mind darkened.

And in that moment, Anjali made a silent vow—

She would take revenge on Arav.

Chapter 12 – Shadows of Revenge

Anjali sat rigid in her office chair, her back straight as steel, her jaw tight, her eyes burning with humiliation. The memory of Arav walking away with Sana played on an endless loop in her mind. She had confessed with boldness, poured her heart into words, even humbled herself by kneeling before him—and yet, he had brushed her aside as though she were nothing.

Worse, he had turned to Sana. Calmly. Naturally. As if Sana belonged at his side.

Anjali's pride, the very shield she had always carried, was shattered. But beneath the sting of rejection, something darker began to grow. He cannot treat me like this. I won't let him.

She stared at her own reflection in the glass window beside her desk. The faint outline of her face seemed almost foreign—her usual charm replaced with a hard, cold determination. "If he wants to ignore me," she whispered to herself, "then I'll give him a reason to regret it. He may be successful, intelligent, admired... but I know exactly how to hurt him."

Meanwhile, across the office, Arav and Sana walked together toward the parking lot. Sana's steps were light, but her heart raced wildly. She could not erase the image of Anjali kneeling before Arav, nor the fear that gripped her in that moment. Yet what stayed with her even more was the way Arav had chosen her instead—steady, calm, without a trace of hesitation.

A quiet warmth spread through her chest. She glanced sideways at him, her lips curving into a faint smile. He could have entertained Anjali's plea. He could have faltered. But he didn't. He turned to me.

Arav, for his part, kept his expression composed. But within, the encounter still lingered. He had rejected Anjali clearly, almost harshly, yet he had done so to protect the fragile balance he was beginning to build with Sana. His gaze shifted toward her briefly, reassuring himself that she was fine—that she knew where she stood in his world.

Back in her office, Anjali drummed her manicured nails against the polished surface of her desk. Her mind spun like a storm, weaving plans born of pride and vengeance. He thinks he can dismiss me. He thinks he can hand his attention to her without consequence. Fine. But he will notice me, one way or another. And if Sana dares to get in the way... she'll suffer too.

The evening sun dipped low, painting the sky in dusky hues of pink and violet. In the parking lot, Arav opened the car door for Sana. She slid inside, her smile tender but her emotions still tangled—jealousy, relief, and a fragile hope intertwining in her heart.

As the car moved through the quiet city streets, Sana leaned back and studied Arav's calm profile. A silent promise formed in her heart. Whatever Anjali tries, whatever storm she brings—I won't lose him. Not now.

And somewhere in the building they had left behind, Anjali's shadow grew darker, her determination sharpening into a dangerous vow. For her, this was not the end. It was only the beginning.

Chapter 13 – The Unspoken Fear

The office was buzzing with its usual chaos, but Sana's eyes darted restlessly across the floor. Arav's desk was empty. She frowned, checking again, but his chair remained unoccupied. A strange unease settled in her chest.

When she asked around, someone whispered that Arav had taken a half day.

Half day? But why? Sana's heart began to race. A few hours later, she overheard another piece of news—that he had submitted a leave application for several days. Her curiosity deepened into worry. Something wasn't right.

Unable to stop herself, Sana went straight to Ram's cabin. "Hi, Ram," she began, her voice tight, "Arav isn't anywhere. Where is he?"

Ram looked up from his laptop, casually replying, "He's at his place. Took half a day off."

Sana leaned forward, her voice lowering, betraying her nervousness. "But why? Why did he suddenly take leave for so many days?"

Ram hesitated, then shrugged. "I don't know everything. But... I heard someone sent him a wedding invitation."

Sana blinked. "Wedding invitation? Who sent it?"

Ram sighed. "Maybe his ex. To show him she's happy without him."

The words struck Sana like a blade. She froze, her mind spinning. Siya... The thought of Arav returning to his hometown, meeting her again—her chest tightened painfully. She forced a smile at Ram, thanked him, and walked back to her desk.

But she couldn't work. Her pen hovered over paper, her computer screen blurred before her eyes. In her head, dark thoughts whirled. What if Arav forgives her? What if they meet again, and all his old feelings return? What if he leaves me...?

She whispered to herself under her breath, "No... no, stop thinking like this. Arav would never let Siya close again. But still... what if? Ahhh, what should I do? I'm going mad!"

Her decision was made before she realized it. She too applied for a half day and left the office, her feet carrying her straight to Arav's apartment.

Her finger trembled slightly as she pressed the doorbell.

A moment later, the door opened. Arav stood there, surprised but calm. "Sana? You're here? What happened? Everything fine?"

"Yes," Sana replied quickly, too quickly. "Everything's fine."

He gave her a soft smile. "Okay... come in. Sit."

She stepped inside and her heart skipped a beat—his suitcase lay open on the bed, half packed. Her chest tightened. "Arav," she said slowly, "are you going somewhere?"

"Yes," he replied matter-of-factly. "I'm going back home."

Sana's face fell. "Why? What happened? Why suddenly?"

Arav zipped a bag pocket and answered, "Someone's missing me... and invited me to her wedding."

The word wedding hit Sana like thunder. She swallowed hard. "Who is calling you? Tell me."

Arav glanced at her and sighed. "Siya's friend. The one who revealed the truth about Siya to me. She's getting married, and she invited me. So I thought... I'll also meet my family."

Sana's pulse hammered in her ears. "If you meet Siya at the wedding... what will you do then?"

Arav's expression turned distant. "She'll definitely come. She's her best friend."

Sana's voice rose, almost pleading. "No... you can't just go like this!"

Arav looked at her, puzzled. "Why? What's wrong?"

Sana fumbled for words. "I mean... if she tries to come close to you, then?"

Arav chuckled lightly. "No. She won't. She knows me well. I won't let her."

"But she's your first love," Sana pressed, her voice trembling.

Arav's eyes softened. "Yes, she was my first love. But now... everything is over."

Sana bit her lip, her heart still heavy. Arav noticed the tension written all over her face, the way her shoulders stiffened at every mention of Siya. He said gently, "Maybe she just feels guilty. Maybe she wants to apologize."

Sana's head snapped up, her voice sharp with panic. "And then what? Then you'll accept her?!"

Arav smirked playfully. "I don't know..."

Her stomach dropped. But before her thoughts spiraled further, Arav continued, "By the way, I had two tickets. I booked one for Ram, but he can't come for personal reasons. If you don't mind... you could come in his place."

Sana froze. Her heart wanted to leap with joy, but her pride hesitated. "No... how can I come? No, I won't."

Arav shrugged casually. "Okay then. I'll go alone. And if Siya apologizes, I will—"

Before he could finish, Sana blurted out, "Okay, fine! I'm coming!"

Her cheeks flushed, her heart pounding, but her eyes shone with determination. She would not let Siya get even an inch closer to Arav. Not now, not ever.

Chapter 14 – The Train Journey

Sana had applied for several days of leave, citing her illness as the reason. Soon after, she and Arav reached the railway station, ready to board the train.

They climbed inside, scanning the compartment for their berths. Just then, Arav made a sudden decision—he canceled Ram's berth and arranged a new ticket directly from the ticket collector. Sana noticed this but remained quietly happy inside; the thought of traveling alone with Arav filled her with joy.

As they settled in, Arav turned toward her with gentle concern.

"If you need anything, just tell me. I'll bring it for you, okay?"

Sana nodded with a soft smile. "Yes."

The day passed slowly, and as the train moved further into the journey, the sun began to sink, painting the sky with hues of orange and red before giving way to darkness. After dinner, both prepared to rest on their berths.

Late into the night, Sana stirred in her sleep and shifted positions. Her eyes fluttered open, only to realize that Arav was not on his berth. A wave of worry rushed through her. Where has he gone?

Unable to rest, she got up and began searching. A minute later, she spotted Arav standing quietly near the doorway of the coach, lost in thought as the night breeze brushed against him.

Relieved, she rushed to him and, without a second thought, hugged him tightly.

"What are you doing here? I got afraid," she whispered.

Arav looked down at her, surprised. "Why?"

Sana hesitated, then confessed softly, "Actually... I have no habit of traveling alone. That's why I felt scared and... hugged you. Sorry."

Arav gave a faint smile. "It's okay. Go and sleep."

But Sana looked up at him with pleading eyes. "Please come with me... I feel uncomfortable there without you."

For a moment, silence lingered between them. Then Arav's lips curved into a gentle smile.

"Okay, let's go."

And together, they walked back toward their berths, the train carrying them forward into the night.

The train rattled steadily along the darkened tracks, its rhythmic clatter filling the silence of the night. Sana walked back to her berth with Arav by her side. Though she tried to calm herself, her heart was still racing from the sudden fear of not finding him.

They sat together for a moment, the dim yellow light above them casting soft shadows on their faces. Sana hesitated, her fingers nervously twisting the edge of her dupatta.

"Arav..." she whispered, almost as if she feared disturbing the quiet around them.

"Hm?" he looked at her calmly.

"You don't know... tonight I really felt scared. Maybe because I'm not used to being away from home like this. But when I saw you standing there, I don't know what happened... I just hugged you without thinking."

Arav gave a faint smile. "You don't need to explain. Fear is natural. But remember, you're not alone here. I'm with you."

His words carried a warmth that settled her heart. She nodded, but her eyes lingered on him longer than before.

They lay down on their respective berths, yet sleep refused to come easily to Sana. Every time the train jolted, she would glance down at Arav, making sure he was still there. Finally, gathering courage, she whispered softly, "Arav... are you awake?"

"Yes," he replied, turning slightly.

"Can I... sit near you for a while? I just can't sleep."

Arav shifted, making space. "Come."

She climbed down and sat beside him, the two of them gazing out of the window where the moon followed the train faithfully across the sky. For a long while, neither spoke. The silence between them was not empty—it was filled with unspoken comfort.

Finally, Sana said, "I don't know why... but with you, I feel safe. Like nothing can hurt me."

Arav looked at her, his expression softening, but he remained quiet. He didn't want to mislead her, nor did he want to break the fragile trust forming between them. Instead, he simply said, "Then don't worry. Just rest. Tomorrow is a long day."

She leaned her head lightly on his shoulder, closing her eyes. The train moved ahead into the night, carrying with it not just two travelers, but the beginning of something neither of them had fully realized yet.

Chapter 15 – The Wedding Confrontation

The wedding venue was alive with music, laughter, and the scent of fresh flowers. Lights twinkled all around as guests moved about, preparing for the grand ceremony.

Arav and Sana stepped inside together. Almost immediately, they were greeted by Lovely—the bride and Siya's closest friend.

"Welcome, brother. Thank you so much for coming," Lovely said warmly, her face glowing with bridal joy.

Arav smiled politely. "Congratulations, Lovely."

Her eyes shifted curiously toward Sana. "And she is...?"

Arav replied calmly, "She's my colleague and friend."

Lovely's smile widened as she welcomed Sana too, treating her with the same warmth. Soon, preparations for the rituals resumed, and everyone got busy.

When the time came, Lovely—dressed beautifully in her bridal attire—walked slowly toward the decorated stage. Arav and Sana also approached to congratulate her.

But in that very moment, Siya appeared. Her eyes fell on Arav... then on Sana standing beside him.

She walked straight up to them, her voice sharp.

"Who is she?" she demanded.

Sana turned, equally curious. "And who is she, Arav?"

Arav remained silent, his eyes avoiding Siya completely.

With a small, almost smug smile, Siya spoke directly to Sana.

"I'm his first love. We madly loved each other once."

She looked at Arav, expecting him to confirm it. "Tell her, Arav."

But Arav simply walked past, not uttering a single word.

Sana's lips curled into a faint smile. "Thank you, Siya."

Siya blinked, confused. "Thank me? Why? I don't even know you."

Sana's voice turned firm yet graceful. "Yes, we don't know each other. But still, I'm thankful to you—for leaving Arav. Because of you, he is with me today."

Siya's face tightened. "What rubbish! Arav will never love you. He still loves me."

Sana nodded slowly. "Probably it's true... maybe a part of him still loves you. But that will not continue anymore. You were his past. I will be his present and his future."

Siya's voice trembled with bitterness. "You don't know him. You can't handle his anger, his restrictions, or even his over-care. You'll leave him just like I did. He won't allow you to talk to other men. He won't allow you to wear western clothes—he is a completely traditional man. That's why I left him. I couldn't live with such old-fashioned thinking."

But Sana laughed softly, her eyes shining with conviction.

"I will never wear western dresses if he doesn't like them. Because he loves me, he has the right to take decisions for me—what kind of clothes I should wear, what's right for me. And if he gets angry, I'll calm him down. I'll search for the reason behind his anger. But I will never leave him like you did, for such silly reasons.

Arav is a gold-hearted man, someone who loves with his whole soul. Very few men love like him. And because of that, I will never let him go. Siya, you lost a diamond in search of gold. That is your bad luck. Arav is mine now."

Siya's face paled. Her pride shattered, regret clawed at her heart. She realized how foolishly she had thrown away someone so rare. Silently, she cursed herself.

Sana, without waiting for her response, turned away. Her eyes searched the crowd until she found Arav standing outside, away from the noise, under the open sky.

She approached him gently. "What happened? What are you doing out here?"

Arav turned his head slightly, his expression unreadable. "Nothing. Just needed some fresh air."

And beside him, Sana stood quietly—her heart full of unshakable determination that no shadow from his past would ever take him away from her.

Chapter 16 – A Confession Under the Stars

The night air was cool, the wedding music muffled in the distance. Sana stood beside Arav, her heart pounding, thoughts swirling like restless winds. Finally, she gathered her courage.

"Arav... if you don't mind, can I say something?"

Arav glanced at her with calm eyes. "Of course. Go ahead."

Sana inhaled deeply. "Till when will you keep yourself stuck in the past—stuck in those painful memories? You have to move on, Arav. Start living as a happy person again."

Arav's lips curved into a faint, bitter smile. "I'm not stuck in the past, Sana. But tell me—how do I forget that she left me for another man? Do you know what that does to a man? It kills his trust. That's why men like me end up with... trust issues. Because of girls like her."

Sana's voice softened. "Maybe. But not everyone is the same. You can't paint all with one brush."

Arav shook his head. His voice carried the weight of old wounds. "Do you know what she used to say to me? She always said, 'Arav, I'll never leave you. If you ever leave me, I'll die alone, but I'll never love another man.' And after all those promises, she walked away. Tell me, Sana—how can I ever trust love again?"

For a long moment, silence stretched between them. The only sound was the faint rustling of trees in the night breeze.

Finally, Sana took a step closer. She swallowed hard, then gently reached for his hand. Her fingers trembled as they laced with his.

"I don't know when or how," she whispered, her voice thick with emotion, "but I fell in love with you, Arav. I want you with me every moment, in front of my eyes. The day Anjali came to you, my heart burned with jealousy. I can't stop it—I really love you. So much."

Her eyes glistened as she looked into his. "I'll always do whatever you ask me to. Just... don't push me away."

Arav tilted his head, a teasing glint in his eyes. "Sana... but there's something I need to tell you."

Her heart skipped. "What?"

He smirked playfully. "Do you remember the day you came to my room, when I was packing my bag?"

"Yes," Sana replied cautiously. "So what?"

"Well," Arav said dramatically, "after you left, Anjali also came to my room."

Sana froze. Her face turned pale. "What? Why did she come? What happened then?"

Arav suppressed a grin. "She held my hand—"

Sana's eyes flared with jealousy. "What?!" she whispered, anger bubbling. "If she dared... I'll kill her."

Arav continued with a fake seriousness. "Then... she placed her hand on my shoulder and started kissing—"

Before he could finish, Sana pulled away, eyes brimming with tears. "Enough! That means you love Anjali, not me?" Her voice cracked as she cried, "I'm leaving, Arav. I'll never disturb you again."

But before she could take another step, a loud laugh escaped from Arav's lips. He clutched his stomach, laughing openly.

Sana's eyes widened in disbelief. "You... you're laughing? On me?"

Still chuckling, Arav said, "Sana, relax. I was joking! Nobody came to my room that day."

Her jaw dropped. "Youuuuu!! How dare you? Do you have any idea how afraid and sad I just felt? What kind of joke is this?"

Her tears spilled, but this time, in a mix of anger and relief. Without thinking, she threw her arms around him, hugging him tightly.

"You're so bad, Arav," she sobbed against his chest.

Arav's smile softened. He wrapped his arms around her, his voice low and soothing. "I'm sorry. I shouldn't have cracked such a joke."

As she clung to him, crying her heart out, he stroked her back gently. In that moment, beneath the vast night sky, something unspoken bound them closer than ever before.

Chapter 17 – A New Beginning

After returning from the wedding they had attended, Sana introduced Arav to her parents. With a shy smile and quiet confidence, she held his hand as they stood before them. Arav, with honesty in his voice, spoke about their love—how it had grown slowly, how it had healed him, and how deeply he respected their daughter.

Her parents listened carefully, their eyes softening with each word. It didn't take long for them to see the sincerity in Arav's eyes. With warmth, they accepted him as their own.

Back in Delhi, Arav sat with his family too, sharing his heart. He spoke about Sana, her kindness, and the strength she had given him when he was at his weakest. His family, especially his mother, looked at him with pride. They could see happiness returning to his face after so many years of silence. Without hesitation, they blessed the union.

The two families met, and soon the decision was made—Arav and Sana's marriage was fixed. Joy filled both homes, and for the first time in a long while, Arav felt complete.

Days passed in excitement, and finally, the wedding day arrived. Arav stood tall in his groom's attire, the traditional sherwani embroidered in gold. Nervousness and joy mixed in his heart as he waited on the stage.

And then, Sana appeared. Dressed in a red bridal lehenga, her eyes lowered shyly under the veil, she walked slowly toward him. Arav's throat tightened with emotion—he could hardly believe this moment was real. Sana was radiant, her beauty glowing not just from her attire but from the love in her heart.

When she reached him, Arav extended his hand. Sana placed her delicate fingers into his, and together they stepped onto the stage. In that instant, nothing else mattered—the past pains, the heartbreaks, the long nights of loneliness—they all dissolved. What remained was love, pure and certain.

Their marriage was celebrated with laughter, music, and blessings from everyone around them. It marked not just the union of two souls, but the birth of a new journey.

Two years later, their home echoed with laughter once again. Sana gave birth to twins—a boy and a girl. The children brought immeasurable joy, filling the house with warmth and playfulness. Arav, holding both his children in his arms, felt as though life had finally given him everything he had ever longed for.

With Sana by his side, and their children in his arms, Arav's family was complete.

HAPPY ENDING ☺

Acknowledgement

With heartfelt gratitude, I extend my deepest thanks to everyone who has been a part of the journey of creating Tere Baad.

I sincerely thank my family and friends for their unconditional support, encouragement, and faith in me throughout this project. Their belief has been my strength during every step of this creative journey.

A special thanks to the cast and crew whose dedication, talent, and hard work have given life to this story. Without their contribution, Tere Baad would not have been possible.

I also express my gratitude to all mentors, well-wishers, and industry professionals who guided me and inspired me to bring this vision to the screen.Finally, I thank the audience and readers who continue to support my work. This film is for all those who believe in love, heartbreak, and new beginnings.

— Prashant Bhardwaj

Writer & Creator of Tere Baad

About the Author

Prashant Bhardwaj is a passionate storyteller and writer whose words blend emotion, reality, and imagination. With a deep love for exploring human relationships, his stories often capture the raw beauty of love, heartbreak, and self-discovery.Tere Baad is a reflection of his creative journey—an emotional tale crafted with sincerity and heartfelt expression. Beyond writing, Prashant enjoys music, films, and traveling, which often inspire the depth and authenticity in his narratives.Through his pen name "Achintya Writing," he aspires to connect with readers on a personal level, offering stories that touch hearts and leave lasting impressions.

About the Author

Prashant Bhardwaj is a storyteller at heart, passionate about exploring the complexities of human emotions, love, and relationships. With a deep understanding of heartbreak, hope, and self-discovery, he brings characters to life in a way that resonates with readers across generations.

When he's not writing, Prashant enjoys traveling, listening to music, and observing the small, meaningful moments of everyday life that inspire his stories. Tere Baad is his latest work, reflecting his signature style of heartfelt drama and poignant romance.

Read more at https://www.instagram.com/achintyawritingpage?igsh=MTI0czZ1YjBqcDh6MQ==.

www.ingramcontent.com/pod-product-compliance
Lightning Source LLC
LaVergne TN
LVHW090433210926
848480LV00002B/811

9798232348816